JACK and the BEANSTALK

Modern Publishing
A Division of Unisystems, Inc. / New York, New York 10022

Jack and his mother were poor farmers who lived by selling their crops, until one day when there were no more crops to sell. All they had left of value was their cow, Buttercup.

"Take Buttercup to market today, and sell her," Jack's mother said sadly. "But be sure you get a good price—it's all the money we'll have in the world."

Jack roped Buttercup and took her to town. On the way he met a man sitting by the side of the road. The man offered to trade a magic bean for Buttercup.

Jack took the magic bean quickly, before the man could change his mind!

Later that afternoon Jack returned home, skipping merrily. "Look what I got for Buttercup," he told his mother proudly. "It's a magic bean…"

"How could you be so foolish, child?" his mother scolded. She threw the bean out the window.

Jack awoke at dawn the next day. When he looked out the window he saw that a tree had sprouted from the bean!

The stalk grew way up into the sky, far beyond the clouds, and passed the birds flying overhead. In fact, Jack couldn't see the top of the beanstalk, so he decided to climb it.

Holding on tightly, Jack climbed higher and
higher until he could see the entire village
below him…and above, he saw a castle floating
in the clouds!

"Hello," Jack shouted as he reached the castle door. When it opened, Jack was amazed. A washerwoman stood before him but she was a giant!

"Oh good, a boy to do my work for me," she said. "Mind my master doesn't find you or he'll eat you for dinner."

Curiously, Jack followed her inside.

Moments later, the castle shook under Jack's feet.

"Oh no, here comes the master," said the fearful washerwoman. "You'd better hide." Jack ran behind the bricks in the fireplace.

"Fee-fi-fo-fum,
I smell the blood of a runty one!
Be he live or be he dead,
his bones I'll grind to make my bread!"

A monstrous giant entered the room and Jack trembled. "I smell a boy," the giant yelled at the washerwoman.

"There's no boy here, sir," she said timidly.

"Better not be, or else. Bring me my gold NOW," he commanded.

After counting his gold, the mean giant fell
asleep. Jack crept up onto the table and ran off
with a sack of coins for his mother.

"Look, Mother, we're rich," Jack said
happily. Then he told her about the beanstalk,
the enchanted castle and the ferocious giant.

But the gold was soon spent, so Jack climbed
the beanstalk again, hoping to find more of the
ogre's treasure.

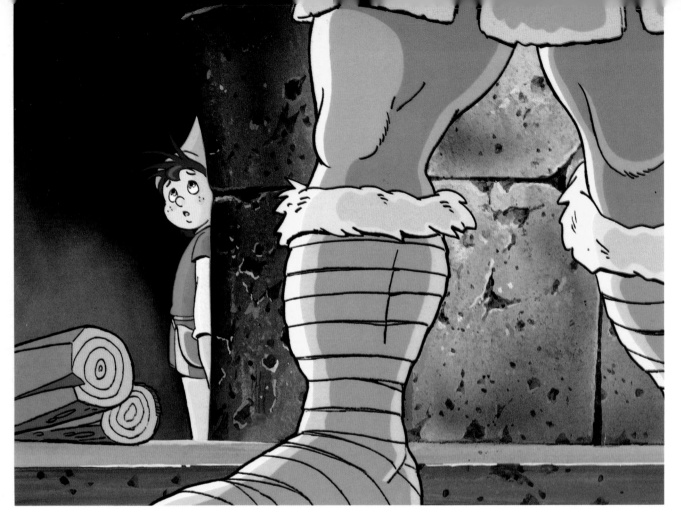

No sooner was Jack in the castle than he heard,

"Fee-fi-fo-fum,
I smell the blood of a runty one!
Be he live or be he dead,
his bones I'll grind to make my bread!"

Jack hid while the brute searched nearly everywhere.

"Bring me my hen NOW," demanded the
giant tyrant, of the washerwoman. Once again,
the giant sat at his table, this time with a
squawking hen upon it. To Jack's surprise he
saw the hen lay an egg of solid gold!

When the wretched giant fell
asleep, Jack took the hen and hurried
back down the beanstalk.

But when the hen died, Jack
climbed way up the beanstalk to
the castle yet again.

"Bring me my harp NOW," he
heard the miserable giant order.
The meek washerwoman brought
a golden harp that told the giant
the secrets of the universe.

When the beastly giant fell
asleep, Jack crawled onto the table
and grabbed the harp from within
an inch of the monster's hand!

"Master, Master!" called the harp as Jack ran away with it. The giant woke up and saw Jack.

Enraged, the giant chased Jack to the beanstalk, waving his spiked bat furiously and narrowly missing Jack with every *crash!*

Jack ran to the beanstalk and began to climb down. The angry giant was right behind and getting closer.

"Mother, Mother, bring an axe!" shouted
Jack as he reached the bottom of the beanstalk.
His mother came running to save her son from
the vicious giant.

Jack chopped through the stalk. He barely got out of the way before the giant crashed to the ground at his feet. The earth shook so from his landing that Jack was thrown up into the air and the giant fell into a deep hole, never to be seen again.

With the wise advice of the all-knowing harp,
Jack and his mother became rich and never
wanted for anything ever again.